I Wish

by Miriam Sklar

ISBN: 978-1-338-75079-9
Illustrated by John Lund

Published by Scholastic Inc., 557 Broadway, New York, NY 10012

10 9 8 7 6 5 4 68 25 26 27/0

Printed in Jiaxing, China. First printing, January 2021.

I wish for a gown.

I wish for a crown.

I wish for a ring.

I wish for a swing.

I wish for a wig.

I wish for a pig.

I wish for wings!